nunt

MINGUS TOURETTE

Foreword by Marvin Gander

zygote **publishing**

National Library of Canada Cataloguing in Publication

Tourette, Mingus
Nunt / Mingus Tourette ; foreword by Marvin Gander.

Poems.
ISBN 0-9734458-0-7

I. Title.

PS8639.O97N86 2004 C811'.6 C2004-900826-9

Design by Geoff Kramer
Photography by A. Tate Young
First Printing 2004

Printed in Canada

For more information on Zygote Publishing, or to order more fine publications, visit www.zygotepublishing.com

For more information about the work of Geoff Kramer, visit www.perpetualnotion.ca

To learn more about Mingus Tourette or to read his regular column, *The Daily Mingus*, visit www.nunt.com

for Nat.

table OF CONTENTS

FOREWORD

FOREWORD

I had been ghostwriting a memoir for several months, when I decided to pick up extra freelance work to sustain me during the inevitable revisions. After a few slow days of fruitless searching, a helpful colleague directed me to a small Canadian literary magazine that needed an impartial journeyman writer. The editors wanted someone to conduct a series of interviews with a poet who was in the midst of creating a long set of experimental writings. The poet was Mingus Tourette and the series was his doomed experimental novel, *Divinity*. Before accepting, I asked for a short biography and a sample of his writing. The senior editor presented this as an example of both:

mt BIO

writer &

vociferous atheist
polygamy advocate
sodomite & womanizer

a hard drinking
volatile son of a bitch
who might just do for Canadian poetry
what jet planes do for skyscrapers

Mingus Tourette
Emphatic Graphomaniac
Chronic Neologist
Thanaphobic Bastard
Purveyor of Fine Apostasy
Effervescent Fuckaroo
&
Notorious Drunkard, Esquire

Although I had misgivings about the project, the editor invited me to his office to introduce me to Tourette. After no further freelance leads materialized, I consented to meet the writer and consider the project. Two icy January days later, I drove an associate professor's car to the magazine's downtown office. When I arrived, Tourette was already present and he was loudly protesting the editor's rejection of a new story. Although it was early in the afternoon, Tourette appeared to be drunk. His speech was littered with obscenities, his gestures were overwrought, and he seemed to be on the verge of falling over.

As best I could gather from the conversation, Tourette had written a story that he thought was critical to the reader's understanding of his entire body of work. Tourette believed it should be published immediately, although the editor thought otherwise. He was inclined to believe the magazine did not need anything else from Tourette when it was owed thirty-three installments of *Divinity* in the near future. Once Tourette realized the editor was not going to publish his story, he shrugged. Though we had never been introduced, he turned to me and said, "If you're Gander, let's get the fuck out of this cocksucking bughatch and get a drink." He crumpled the story in his hands and walked out of the office, gesturing grandly to an unseen audience as he left. The editor smirked and returned to his keyboard, making it clear that the decision to play along was all mine.

I followed Tourette out the front door and into the bitter cold. He had smoothed out the crumpled paper and was reading the story to himself. He noted my presence, started walking, and led us down the street to a nearby pub. As we entered, we passed a sign indicating knives were to be left at the door. Once through the metal detector, Tourette pointed to a table and left me waiting as he went to buy drinks from the bartender, whom he seemed to know. He returned with a couple of pints of foul-coloured lager, handed one of them to me, and pushed the wrinkled story into my hands. He leaned back in his seat, cradled his drink, and stared off into the distant regions of the bar. It appeared there would be no conversation until I had finished reading the rejected work, which I found helped me understand Tourette and his writing.

Tourette may be crass and reading his work for the first time may feel like a violation, but the more one reads and understands it, the more his humanity becomes apparent. I believe that a writer's work is his best introduction, and so I would like to present Tourette's story:

Used to drive an '84 Buick Skylark
and there was one summer
back before ever meeting America
when Nat and I were still deeply entrenched
in each other's flesh

when I'd never thought about dragging myself
across the country in a drunken haze

and the idea of driving that Skylark
to Mexico was a real and somewhat
titillating possibility
for me and Nat

the car itself was shit brown
with rust throughout and looked generally
like hell all over

but that thing had six big valves
and decent tires
and it could hit a hundred miles an hour going down hill
if there was no need to stop quickly

'Cause if there had been
and there was later
those dirty old brakes would have never held

Which they didn't

And when the time came for them to work
and they didn't
and Nat's belly was crushed by the shitty old seat belt
that only went around the waist

and she split her forehead on the dash

there wasn't much Mingus could do
except watch her bleed on the insides
watch her belly swell

as it was supposed to
slowly
over nine months
but not like that
not in a matter of minutes

and fill that uterus with blood
and choke out that unborn Sara, or Sarah, or Sera

however it was to be spelled

until a trucker picked them up on the road
desperate and broken

and that old trucker drove them away
from the smashed up Buick
and up to the hospital
even though it was too late
and away from unborn Sarah

and somewhere before the time it would be possible
for Mingus to afford to drive another car
and all he would remember
about driving
would be that old Skylark

and how it looked as he sat
in the back of the truck with his young wife
who was maybe hemorrhaging
and how it would feel in the near future

when that car was pushed into a car graveyard
when he and Nat would stand on the edge of a cliff
to pour a thimble full of ashes into a canyon

she would weep and he would stare stoically
and only shake on the inside.

There was one summer before all that
when Mingus drove that Skylark
and dreamed about Mexico
and smiled

When I finished, Tourette looked at me expectantly, raised a single eyebrow and grinned. He said, "And now that you know, let's get into it. Let's talk *Divinity*." And so we did. And so we would for the next nine months, until Tourette decided to abandon the project and start working on *Nunt*.

Divinity was a modified stream-of-consciousness experiment loosely based on Dante's *Divine Comedy*.[1] It was filled with brilliant images but, as far as anyone could tell, there were only a handful of interested readers. During one of our monthly interviews, Tourette and I discussed the project at length, and I listened as he considered abandoning what he thought was becoming an unreadable Joycean nightmare. He feared the work was marginalized by its new form, that it was not telling a story and, most importantly, that he could find no emotional heart in the work. He valued the relationship between the two main characters, but found he was writing what he called "a violent imagist exercise, Jack's [2] version of the abyss, and nothing else..." Tourette wanted to write more muscular poetry like that of Purdy, Whitman, or Miller, writers who were, in Tourette's eyes,

[1] In *Divinity*, Mingus Tourette took on the role of Dante, while a black spearman named Kob replaced the poet Virgil, who led Dante through the *Divine Comedy*.

[2] Jack Kerouac, well known for his novel, *On the Road*, but also known to poets as an excellent dharma, haiku and zen writer.

> [a]ll cock and muscle, men who could work with a pickaxe all day, drink all night, fuck all morning and take that last moment before sleep came crashing in to catch that day and squeeze it down into something beautiful. 'Cause that's fucking poetry. I don't care what anyone says these days. Fuck the intellectual exercises. Poetry is still about cunt, it is still about death, it is still about love, and it is still about fucking with hot Catholic bitches 'til they squeeze all the God out of you.
>
> ***Divinity* Interview #5**

We discussed *Divinity*'s style and I suggested shortening the remaining Cuntos to a more manageable format and length. The Cunto was Tourette's version of a Canto, which has evolved into the Nunto. For centuries, the Canto has been used as a division within a long poem, such as Dante's *Divine Comedy* or Spenser's *The Faerie Queene*. Tourette's rationale for developing and using the Cunto was explained in our first *Divinity* interview:

> [C]unto is the rhythm of fucking, it's the break in theme, it's the division in a poem; 'cause it all changes within the fuck, it changes with different women, it changes all the time, when you're just about to come compared to when you first slide it in, it's about rhythm and breaks and different passages of time. Cunt governs everything, really. We all base our whole lives on it. Quest for it, fight for it, lie for it, break heads for it. So why not have it govern a whole poem? A whole novel? Cunt is life and, of course, life rules poetry. What else would a poem be about, except life? Except cunt?
>
> ***Divinity* Interview #1**

Tourette contended, however, that it was not just the form that was bothering him. He could not shake the paradoxical fact that he was an atheist writing about a journey through the nine levels of the Catholic Abyss. Hell was something he no longer believed in, and though he stared into the Abyss, nothing stared back. As we had come to know each other quite well by that time, I felt comfortable pressing him to define the material he wanted to write. He was unresponsive at first, so I rephrased the question and asked him to define his own abyss. There was a long silence, and he said,

> Nat. And the two years after, (laugh). Fuck, Marvin, that's all I write about. What else am I writing about? Those two years. That's what I write when I'm not writing this thing. Drinking and writing and hating God and walking and Dostoevsky. And Nat. Fucking Christ, Nat. Fucking Christ...
>
> ***Divinity* Interview #5**

Tourette occasionally spoke to me about the events that led to the disintegration of his marriage. As far as I understand, the accident resulted in a void between Tourette and his wife, which led to depression, drinking, and years of fighting. They tortured each other until their friends and families advised them that the marriage should end. They spent a year divorcing each other, but even when it was finalized, they continued to live together in a purgatory that neither one could seem to escape. Describing his actions as, "the only way [he] could think to end it without killing her or [him]self," Tourette finally walked out the front door, bought a bus ticket, and fled the country.

After leaving, Tourette travelled alone across the States for almost two years, making occasional sojourns back to Canada. During his travels, he scribbled poems and anecdotes on napkins or bus tickets. Most of the segments were written in roadside diners after drunken brawls, and many of them he cannot remember writing. He kept little else from that period besides those scraps of paper and, after he abandoned *Divinity*, he returned to them as a basis for this book.

In essence, *Nunt* begins on the day Tourette left Nat for the last time and "drank, smoked, cussed, and fucked"[3] his way across America, trying desperately to discover a way to forget his wife.

> [I find myself]
> finally driven to ask
> an Egyptian druggist
> rumoured to be an atheist
> or an alchemist
>
> confiding in him one night
> lost deep in the opium dens of Chinatown
> asking, with sleepless eyes
>
> what do I take
> for hallucinations
>
> or better yet
>
> what the fuck do I take to stop seeing ghosts

Nunto Thirty-four

Nunt is commentary on the people Mingus drank with, slept with, and fought with as he dragged himself from city to city. *Nunt* is criti-

[3] nunto one, line 7.

cism of the American people and their government, though it is often through them that he sees himself. Incidents in the book can be bitter and forthright,[4] but many of the stories are subtly damning, portraying Americans as he encountered them.[5] *Nunt* is condemnation of the xenophobia, stupidity, fear, violence, and religion that he observed, which forced him to ask the question,

> whatever does it mean to be American?
> besides
> a jihad against one's self?
>
> **Nunto Fifty**

Tourette's undisguised loathing for religion spills into his writing with the undeniable rancour of a violently reformed Christian. Tourette often refers to people as "shaved apes wearing ties"[6] and gives the impression that he would like to see all religions abandoned in the same manner that he abandoned *Divinity*. He abhors evangelists,[7] detests fundamentalists,[8] and delights in finding new ways to infuriate the religious rank and file.[9] But no matter how much vitriol he spews at Americans and organized religion, he reserves the worst criticism for Nat and himself.

> She was a cock fiend
> cock hungry
> cock drunk is more like it
> and I mean that as a compliment
>
> **Nunto Nineteen**

> I say, it is easy to see
> how that man could beat
> his ex-wife and her lover
> to death
> with a piece of timber
> in a park
> in clear daylight
> in front of a horrified crowd
>
> simply said,
> I empathize with everyone these days
>
> fistfighting, indeed
> we got to be at the murdering age by now
>
> **Nunto Thirty-nine**

[4] nunto two, lines 53-59.
[5] nunto twelve, lines 9-22.
[6] nunto sixty-three, lines 8-14.
[7] nunto twenty-one, lines 7-18.
[8] nunto four, lines 12-37; nunto eight, lines 8-12.
[9] nunto sixteen, lines 9-25.

During the two years Tourette was travelling, he returned home on a few desperate occasions in an effort to reconcile with Nat. Each attempt left the situation worse than before, and every time the marriage dissolved, he left town determined to do whatever it would take to finally rid her from his system.

> [A]nd me with a real fucking death wish
> to get there
> get away from you
> been staring off bridges and taunting oncoming trucks
> been out all night walking the streets
> fast
> under the green haze
>
> looking for a huge Iranian whore
> who goes by the name Therese
>
> I wanted her to crush me
> to lie on me like a dead animal
> and force the air from my lungs
>
> she'd do it, too.
> she's into shit like that
> she would respect a man's wish
> to die beneath her

Nunto Sixty-two

After two years of living in cheap hotels, walking the streets, and pushing the drink as close to the edge as he could, he returned home exhausted and somewhat purged. Today, Nat and Tourette are properly estranged and they do not keep in touch. He still talks about her on occasion, but it is sad and wistful and angry when he does.

Nunt is about Nat. It is about Mingus Tourette. It is about the two of them, together and apart. It is about how one can find something beautiful and disgusting, and aspire to recreate it truthfully for others to share. It is about sex, drugs, prostitutes, buggery, fist fighting, murder, apostasy, God, death, literature, jazz, rock and roll, scat, zen, and madness. It is about losing one's self in the ocean and letting one wash up on whatever shore that will call one home. And sometimes, whether you would admit it or not, Mingus, it is even about love, no matter how malformed and destructive and mercurial it may seem.

> [S]he won't ever say it
> but there is a disgusting beauty
> to our soiled love sheets
> in the afternoon sun

Nunto Sixty-three

Marvin Gander
February 1, 2004

BOOK I

nunto ONE

broken pavement
the slow decay of the city's enamel
sharp reminder
of the time

24 & hard
living in exile
I drank smoked cussed and fucked
my way across the old colonies

and kept on waking up
face down and cold
in the morning streets
of a castigating and alien land

and no matter how debauched
how bloodied and how anonymous
myself and my virulent whores were

no matter how many times I shattered

I was
never far enough from the old spectre
that haunted me

such is what the drunkards allegedly call love
and the absence of it

nunto TWO

blind drunk and no good for throwing em
probably going to get curbed out here

but I just had to start it
a good old fashioned cursing competition
in the parking lot
a little fist fight preamble
between me and this shit sniffing redneck
who calls himself the southern bard
just had to start it
because I really cannot brook anyone saying
William fucking Shakespeare could kick the hell out of
my man Henry Miller

nobody calls Henry a pussy
while I'm still standing
so I start out with a little jab
to see what he's got under his skirt

I say, simply
You fuck the fuck off with your Billy Shakespeare
he was a Victorian fruitcake and you know
Henry would have made him his bitch

To which he retorts
in a suspect
rather unoriginal form

No
you fuck the fuck off
or I'll rip off your head and shit
down your throat

and that dooms him
puts the mark of the dumb upon him
allowing me to lay into it
and start preaching with a little brimstone

Well, boys.
I think we've all heard that one before
and I can tell you right now, he's got nothing else.
So son
I'm going to give you and your southern Gentlemen here
a much needed lesson in how to curse
before I kick you down to the pavement and leave you
cockless in the gutter
so your tongues won't be completely useless
you cunnilingually deficient Texan retard bastards

why don't you fuck the fuck off before I beat the hell out of you
like Johnny Goddamn Cash and Merle Shit Kicking Haggard
breaking into your trailer at six in the morning
with baseball bats and four gallons of kerosene

why don't you fuck the fuck off before I rape you
in this here parking lot
cut you open like Sharon Tate
and paint your Camaro with pig's blood

why don't you fuck the fuck off before I sodomize your poodle
shave your mullet
diddle your little sister
steal your combine
and burn down your church

why don't you fuck the fuck off before I nail you up on a cross
like the KKK crucifying Malcolm Motherfucking X
like a Virginian governor throwing the switch on a child fucker
like a Southern president bombing ragheads
with that righteous wrath
only an American can have when he's killing Muslims

that's right
fuck off like a Baptist minister burning books written to inflame

by god hating drunkards like me

so why don't you fuck the fuck off or
I'll kick you so fucking hard in the sack
you'll find out what your own lousy cum tastes like

and with that last gravedigger
I whisper a little prayer to old Henry
wishing he was there
'cause my patron saint would have a hell of a haymaker

and I up end a bottle of whiskey
and come out swinging

nunto THREE

the fact remains
that no matter how beautiful
or dignified a Woman is

how possessed of grace

she still looks like a donkey
when she's sucking Cock

not that it minds me

nunto FOUR

the kind of town where people
invariably ride their snowmobiles to church
in winter

somehow arrived with my Lloyd
who isn't really supposed to be practicing
but what the fuck
he's a Lloyd and therefore

well above the law
especially back woods hick law
and he's wearing some fancy jewelry and a fox fur wrap
I know he swindled off some poor old widow

which is good for the clown show that he's putting on
a quick fix for all your woes
it's got something to do with insurance
greased up with a little god talk

but I know how this is ending already
us, on the third night
the audience with hands full of rotten tomatoes
and some with shivs fashioned out of sharpened crucifixes

and we're leaving in a hurry with more than we came with
on the back of a stolen snowmobile
or if it comes to it
somebody's horse
but what the hell

these people are all related
and if they'd been here since Judas cashed in
they'd all look exactly the same
no colour no race no love
always feuding and hanging blacks and worshipping
ridiculously and they ain't skinny
so fuck em and their buck teeth breeding

we're out of here with our old lady silver and hay dollars
pig money and such on the back of a stolen mare
me, the lloyd, hunter and huckleberry
and if they cry hunger in the night

let em eat god

nunto FIVE

pants down around the ankles
my feet wrapped about the iron bars
as I stick my ass out
over the edge of the balcony

some fat old broad in the bedroom
who knows that the great equalizer
amongst women
is the ability to suck a good Cock

and me with a bottle at my feet
nine stories up
reading Charlie Bukowski
chuckling
leaning backwards over the rail

defecating on the city

nunto SIX

I don't know why
I'm preaching to this young gangbanger
calling himself a mack
calling himself Duke Warback

why I'm telling him how to run his game

maybe
it's 'cause he's doing it all wrong
and I like to see the game played straight

Jesus, he got the girls on drugs
shooting up other players' tracks
slapping bitches till they bleed
getting into fights
knocking everything in sight

and his clothes
I say, motherfucker, you call that a hat?

I say
Pimp! Mo'fucking Mack Pimp!
You got to play the game more like Slim
you know, the Iceberg!

and he looks at me
eyes saying he don't know the Grand Daddy
and I shake my head
'cause a young hustler don't know goddamn Iceberg Slim

kids these days
and I worry

I mean, maybe it's just because
I like to see the game well played

or maybe

more likely

it's 'cause
I'm in love
with one of his girls

fuck can you do?

nunto SEVEN

Somewhere i read
Anacreon saying

Nature gave to the lion
a chasm of teeth.

a passage whose beauty
should be far beyond me
but it's not

for i am
thin
unattached to any particular social group
compulsively haunting used book stores
prone to minor substance abuse

and
writing without any context
without
any description or future plan

discarding the flowers of speech
on napkins and toilet paper
along the way

nunto EIGHT

"Literature, shiterature."

fifteen beers in and having a hell of a good time
twisting the fuck out of old Doctor Dick's logic
which is infuriating the cunt hairs off of him

he's got the doctorate in talking books
but I got the writers on my shelf
and no matter what his wish

I know what semantics means
and I'm bending him over on irony
white symbolizes death in the East and
Jesus Wept
is the shortest lie in the book

Dick
you're a smart guy
and you can tell me what their intentions and metaphors were
but you can't hold your liquor for shit
and now you're getting frustrated and can't stand up straight
in this heated discussion
'cause you never got drunk on words

not like me
like it says on my card

Mingus Tourette
Emphatic Graphomaniac
Chronic Neologist
Thanaphobic Bastard
Purveyor of Fine Apostasy
Effervescent Fuckaroo
&
Notorious Drunkard, Esquire

so shit in the milk of that, doc

nunto NINE

Jou wadch the ping pong show
baa naa naa show - ping pong
the fucking show - banana
ago go show - chopstick show

agogo gogo agogo go go

taxi driver's singing to me
to himself
doing a little ass jig behind the wheel

high as an albatross
weaving through traffic
dreaming of dancing girls
in some other country

singing a helluva song
and I wish I was
sitting there with him
in that bar - away from here
ogling in wonder and hooting

bugaloo, baby. bugaloo.

nunto TEN

blood soaked sheets
like we just slaughtered a buffalo
and a twinge in my neck
every time
I turn my head
leaving me to count
another goddamn sex injury

that's the last time I support
the full weight of our bodies
with just my neck

while I got encrusted fingers
buried to the knuckles
in her ass

thighs covered in blood
caked on hands and chest
and a smile that looks like
I just ate out
a human sacrifice

I say, K
all these Catholic girls are fucking cannibals

nunto ELEVEN

What's the best way to wake up on a morning like this?

semen on the hands
or
semen on the face?

nunto TWELVE

still hard to believe that
I'm witnessing this
that I've Sawyered my way into
saying grace at this fucking wedding
as the acting Minister

being widely ignored
as the bride was piped in
to the sounds of AC/DC
as the wedding party stood in front
of a garbage can
one by one
and drank beer till
they threw up in it
as one lady told me
she was so happy they were third cousins
and the best man cracked jokes
about sodomy, erections, priests
assholes, sisters and wet dreams

but was booed off stage
not for the jokes, of course,
but for introducing
his nigger bride to be

thinking that after the blessing
I'm gone like Gandhi

'cause these fucking rednecks
are ready for a lynching
in the burnt out asshole of Trauma, America
Home of the Original Squalor Pie

nunto THIRTEEN

trying to suppress a little grin
and show my supposed guilt

for fucking an epileptic
and coming during her seizure

nunto FOURTEEN

in love with a serious ripper
who only strips to Beethoven
some call it a gimmick
though I like to think it shows depth

but every night
I have to tell some fuckwat
at the club
to titter away and leave my woman alone

usually it does it to say
step off, bitch, I've got scars longer than your cock
but this one bugger, a Lloyd in a business suit
keeps returning

so the last night we're in there
I've been stealing cowboys' beers all evening
and I'm completely potted

so I got the gumption when I see him up on perv row
to ask him
with just the right tone between nonchalant
and Chikatilo-like sociopath

Lloyd
You want to wake up
in my bathtub and
look up to see your legs hanging
from my towel rack
and me standing over you
in a lab coat and a welding mask
holding a straight razor?

if not
get the fuck out of here
before I rufie your next drink
and load you into my trunk

wrapped in the
burnt shroud of civility I keep stashed
between the hooker's head and my guns

I wear it like a superhero, you know?

the Lloyd goes white and
either he'll never come back
or the cops will
and it'll all be over in any case

but it had to be done
a man has to protect a treasure like her

for she is immaculately petite
with long black hair that smells fresh
after she washes the smoke and the oil out
and Jesus
she wriggles down that pole during the 9th
in a way that makes my asshole tingle
like my cock's about to blast off into the air
and soar into the sun

BOOK II

nunto FIFTEEN

From somewhere between the
hot dog stand and the blazing bowl
this dyspeptic cunt
from wetworks
has the nerve to tell me
fucking tell me

he's got problems

when I got one dead widow in hand
another on the line
the mail order brides in transit
and two walking corpses
stepping lightly after me

jesus, nat's on a cross
resurrecting herself for a little negro waltz
around the old dance floor
and i'm so broken after a week and a half on the piss
i'm nearing catatonic

so I'm thinking that
after I've balled her snatch inside out
while she's wearing her new gown she bought
at one of those fancy boutiques I shadow

I'm going to have to pop over to K's to hammer one of those
crazy russian bitches
followed by a couple of hours with the widow on 28th
my lonely whore on 4th
and the cop who likes her snapper tickled with the baton

but the problem is
nat finds out I'm juggling while she's in town
I know the crazy bitch has a gun and it's
going to be an abattoir

so don't cry to me about your pregnant daughter
most likely I had nothing to do with it

nunto SIXTEEN

Bloody caesar
bloody mary
bloody nunt

and every other lost drink

What I don't need
is another thigh high innocent
staring starry eyed into the blue
while she's dribbling on my cock

but if it means ploughing untrod earth
and giving a woman of the cross
the wood she needs
call me a martyr

and allow me to set up
a night of polyandrous experimentation
which involves some solipsism on her part
plus myself and a pair of defrocked theologians
because it somehow seems less sinful with former altar boys
who are all quite wonderful about it

and let us hammer her properly
like the carpenter never did

Jesus
how I love your
Nunt

your
Vatican Pink Meat

nunto SEVENTEEN

I knew it was love
the day I said

well bitch, I hope you
like the taste of
ball juice

and she just smiled her sanguine grin
and nearly gnawed
my cock off

slurped it all up
like honey on toast

nunto EIGHTEEN

The privilege
of pissing

beside the bartender
in a place like this

and smelling his after shave
and saying
Good Evening, Sir.

and wondering

what old woman does
he bless this night.

nunto NINETEEN

The way to a man's heart
is through his cock
Worship at that temple
and ye shall succeed

She knew this, Nat, and I know that's
why we stayed together
so long
suffered through all those lacerations

She was a cock fiend
cock hungry
cock drunk is more like it
and I mean that as a compliment

One has to respect a woman
with that kind of thirst

nunto TWENTY

leaving Salt Lake City in a hurry
not the best place for a man of my
particular bent these days

too many virgins and
not enough free flowing liquor
though I have to say
the book of Mormon has provided
some of the best handjobs I've had in a long time

but that doesn't alleviate the fact
that after inciting a temple riot in which
people walked room to room with a chainsaw
cutting holes in the wall
ripped down the spiral oak staircase
burned the pews in the backyard
sawed fireman holes from the second story to the lobby
shat on the altar and
in one inspired moment of rampant drunkenness

they mowed the shag rug

I now estimate
that I am in some trouble with the locals
and definitely
cannot afford another fist fight with a Mormon deacon
no matter the quality of the heavy petting I get
because to the judge and jury and executioners here
I just burned down Zarahemla
and fucked Joseph's wife

Sure, the bitches had it coming, and so did Joseph
but they're still going to kill me and
bury my carbon skeleton beneath their mountain
forever

just me
the lost golden tablets of the angel Moroni
and the truth

nunto TWENTY-ONE

So he's always on that cellphone
that immaculate greased up zoot suit
on the corner of 9th and Main
talking in tongues
shaking hands and taking quick spins
in pimp rides

As far as we all know
that motherfucker
is running Bibles
to the Mormons
the Jews
and the Muslims
on the down low

who says he's selling H?

I mean, maybe he is.
maybe he can find us a horse

or maybe he just pushing more mare's nests
on the easily deluded

nunto TWENTY-TWO

Stranded in a nightclub
full of cocksuckers

with no money
no place to stay
empty gullet and
nothing in my pocket

but two cigarettes
a fake Zippo lighter
a zen phrase book
they found in Yukio Mishima's apartment
after he cut himself open

and a sharpened butterfly knife
i sort of know how to use

thinking

one of you poofters is getting
a mouthful tonight

nunto TWENTY-THREE

Stendahl's hypocrisy
and my own
how I love to read Scarlet and Black with hard liquor in reach
like Cervantes and red wine

but it's the oddity of
living life as though it mattered
when all day, every day
thinking
violent, horrible, sad, tragic death

in all its variations

my own, parents, brother, lover

moving when moving doesn't matter

all the sunshine
vaguely obscured

by the obsidian wall

nunto TWENTY-FOUR

a little club in some
knock off Bourbon street

and through some
unholy miracle
this little Latino on the sax
with horn rimmed glasses and a shoddy goatee
who don't give a fuck
what year it is
and would punch you in the face
if you said

you know son
Thelonius Monk is dead

this kid
lost in the past
bopping and howling on stage
with Mingus and the Duke

playing jazz to murder by

nunto TWENTY-FIVE

Last night
I could not tell
where

your skin ended and
mine began
and now

I've walked from our den
to the steel world
and back
to the dew in the garden remaining

and outside
the pillars of concrete
like sutures
torn by exertion

I am stationary
it is the world
that is spinning away from me

nunto TWENTY-SIX

It takes a long time for a Volkswagen to sink.

That's how he starts the conversation
with eighteen stitches in his belly
no one visiting either one of us
some burn victim screaming down the hall

all I got is the morphine or demerol
and old Vic's stories
an entire life in one sleepless night on the ward

how his daughter got into the cocaine
and cleaned out his entire house
with her cocaine boyfriend

the Volkswagen
the semi-professional prize fighting
the brother who killed himself over gambling debts
and then the light in his eyes
the story about

how he divorced his wife
got lonely
and then moved back in
so they could live together in sin

nodding in the darkness
'cause I know
how much better it is
to fuck your wife
once the rings are safely pawned

nunto TWENTY-SEVEN

One of those fucks where
Miles Davis quit playing
an hour ago

And Us, from door to chair
to floor to top to bottom
to cock to cunt to mouth
to front to back to tit
to ass to hand to face to cunt

and finally coming
like lifting off into
the opening sky

pure unadulterated joy
even, at this moment,
love
which as Freddy says
needs no justification

lie back and shudder
and taste the blood

too weak to stand

nunto TWENTY-EIGHT

Fucking
fucking
fucking
what?

slut?

I'd rather spend
my entire life
drunk
with you

than alone
and sober

don't cry.

it's supposed to be
a compliment

the best

'cause I've
never
spoken truer words

nunto TWENTY-NINE

he's old and he looks
like he could have been a priest
at one point

I mean, he's got a big cross tattooed
on one arm
and a naked madonna servicing Christ
on the other

telling me and K
all about the times

back when I was in the seminary
back when I studied the book of revelations
back when John's letters played roulette with my head
back when I was raping nuns
in Calcutta

oh yes
back when I had
my first sweet taste of nunt

what we can do but shake our heads
in drunken disbelief
at the earnestness
of this unknown neologist

nunto THIRTY

Relax, girl.

It's just like taking a big shit.

Only in reverse.

nunto THIRTY-ONE

Fledgling

shaking like a newborn

it's hard to speak English
after a fuck like that

nunto THIRTY-TWO

From Toronto
to Detroit
to Phoenix
to Los Angeles

it's the same roadside villages
same streetlights
same humming bridges

and every night, in every cheap motel
every homogenous fuck,
i open my eyes wide enough they can't see anymore
and i keep pretending, Nat

it's you sweating on top of me
it's you hitting my chest as you come
it's you kicking me

staring with your mouth open
screaming nothing at dirty walls
in these fucking train stops

nunto THIRTY-THREE

yes

it seemed like a good sort of joke
between the two of us
when I said

I am going to drink twenty-six ounces
of raw absinthe
suck off the green fairy
find out if I can dig up some laudanum
and see what happens

I should need bail money around midnight
bring lloyds and several police

but now i know
i won't be laughing later
'cause at this moment
after the hiss of burning sugar cubes
it's all about the stomach pump
and the violence

yes

it's a bad night
when I'm phoning the hospital
and telling them
to beef up their security
for about 12.30

'cause I'm on my way

nunto THIRTY-FOUR

This fucking city
not unlike old Fyodor and Nikolai's Petersburg
the bureaucrats
the gamblers
and the consumptives

walking fast
with a hatchet and a purpose

a moneylender's blood
and the appearance of Jesus Christ

running a fever now
seeing shades of your naked figure everywhere
no matter what I snort or drink
or hammer into these veins

finally driven to ask
an Egyptian druggist
rumoured to be an atheist
or an alchemist

confiding in him one night
lost deep in the opium dens of Chinatown
asking, with sleepless eyes

what do I take
for hallucinations

or better yet

what the fuck do I take to stop seeing ghosts

BOOK III

nunto THIRTY-FIVE

The whole truck ride, nine hours
this supposed vet's going on about his war and his syndrome
and his pension and his annoying fucking guilt
this Rear Echelon Mother Fucker
sickening me with his rhetoric
and finally I say

You want a fucking war story?

This time about five years ago
I was
working in Cambodia

got pulled over at a border by a fat, greasy looking police inspector
who obviously wanted a bribe, but I wasn't doing anything

wrong

so he shows me a grenade and says I can throw it for ten bucks
and me, who used to toss Molotov Cocktails off overpasses

can't refuse

so he drives me out to this field and
I'm a little afraid he'll just shoot me in the back and take the money
but he's honest, so he hands me the grenade, clips the price tag off
with a pair of field scissors and shows me how to pull the pin
and I pull that fucker and I throw it as hard as I can and
we watch it blow the hell out of the wall of an old barn

it's a satori-like moment

the smoke clears, and we see one forlorn looking
deserted cow inside
who wanders out to inspect the damage

Carpe Diem

the inspector smiles greasy sly grease at me
and digs out another grenade

thirty bucks, he says. American.

nods to the cow

now, there's no one else around but me and him and the cow
and fucked as it, rationalize it - when in Cambodia
but really, I was thinking

when am I ever going to have a chance to kill something this big
like this. with a fucking grenade. ever.

and.

when am I ever going to have a chance to kill
without consequence?

it's a telling question for all of us

but I answer quickly
give him thirty bucks. american.

pull the pin, which makes a funny click
the cow looks as I throw it, but doesn't move 'cause
it only lands close by - doesn't hit him precisely

and he's an inquisitive cow, so he sniffs it

and we watch in curious horror as the cow licks it
at the precise moment it explodes
vapourizes the front half of the cow in a haze of bright red
leaving two legs and a shrivelled udder
to topple gracelessly to the ground

we look around briefly for the tongue
but can't find it

the inspector drives me back to the checkpoint
and we only talk in glances

and later that day I am walking into Vietnam alone
my eyes hurting from the flash
head in a haze
blood still throbbing at the exhilaration
of seeing death at my hand

ears ringing from the sound of bovine murder
which sounds funny, but really

I'm thinking seriously
thank Christ it wasn't an abandoned child
'cause I don't like to think of my answer
to that question

sweet hymn of the killing fields

now that, my unknown soldier,
is a fucking war story

nunto THIRTY-SIX

I saw Shannon Hoon
sitting in an all night diner

tonight

So I walked in, sat beside him

watched him humming and reading from
a book of southern hymns
and I was curious as hell, so
I asked

what's it like?

and he replied
in that soft southern
hippie
voice

'It's harmless.'

there was nothing to reply to that
nothing needed
so we sat and drank coffee

and I listened to him sing his hymns
in his gentle way

nunto THIRTY-SEVEN

the old man
with the wide gin eyes
and the beer notices me
writing in my book and says

in one moment of hard thought
before flowing on

You just do as much
as you can and the sparks
will come off in your wake
and some will glimmer and fade

and others will burn so long
no one will be able to ignore them.

nunto THIRTY-EIGHT

I tell her to take me home
from this late night cricket shack
with the line that I have used

with surprising success

And when I say it, I can tell
it's about to work again.

She's that kind of woman

Well.

It's time for fistfighting or fucking, girl.

One or the other
'cause
I got an urge to draw blood.

nunto THIRTY-NINE

I walk out of vodka
like a clean, sober morning
and old K's still beaking about Nat
so I'm beaking back, serious this time
no more fucking around this thing

are you kidding, K?
maybe back when
we were kids
in the schoolyard

I'd call him out
and beat the hell out of him
in front of everyone

but we're adults
now
so for something like this
it's childish to fight someone

you get mad like this
at this age
and you fucking kill them
break into their room in the night
and shoot them in the head

I say, it is easy to see
how that man could beat
his ex-wife and her lover
to death
with a piece of timber
in a park
in clear daylight
in front of a horrified crowd

simply said,
I empathize with everyone these days

fistfighting, indeed
we got to be at the murdering age by now

nunto FORTY

i don't care how Rimbaud did it

the next time i take it
in the ass

I'm going to insist on rules
no hair pulling
no name calling
no scratching
and
no pissing on my back

either that or more money
Christ, I'm getting that desperate look

i really don't know if i can last
another
season in hell

nunto FORTY-ONE

Nine frat boys
barrelling out of the back of a van
screaming
kickass kickass kike ass kick ass

the words of my crazy Polish fighting coach
in my ears somewhere
'cause he was a dirty fucker and half his conversations
started with

In the ring you do this
but on the street you do this

telling me
you ever get jumped by a bunch of guys and
you got no gun no knife and nowhere to run

you got to fucking kill the first guy
that gets to you
remember, you never punch
hell
you don't even knee the fucker in the balls

you drive your fingers into his eyes like this
so fucking hard
that you can grab one - you cup it from behind
and pull it out

then you rip it off like you're starting a lawnmower
and pop it in your mouth
and crunch it and leave that eye string
hanging down your chin with the jelly squirting out

and come up off the ground like that with your own eyes
rolled back and the blood running down your chest
and scream

I'm going to eat your fucking hearts

and if that doesn't scare them off
or give you space to run
you're fucked
so make sure you do it right the first guy, uh?

and the first guy is there
and what else can i do
but drive them fingers in hard enough
i can feel his brain wriggle when i cut his cord

nunto FORTY-TWO

a sweet young girl
with a yellow sundress

her head full of
fluff and wonder

split open

that beautiful dress
hiked up around her waist

and her head
curdling

injected with ink

nunto FORTY-THREE

We've been sitting in
this booth
for seven hours
talking about
Pierre Trudeau

and taking turns
snorting the lines
off Melvin's
lasagna pan.

it won't be long
before it all goes
violent

can't trust
these fucking liberals

nunto FORTY-FOUR

another worn out old whore
a blind diseased albino wonder
from Africa
named Shalokan

who coughs all the time
makes people wait for her to speak
and is known to take it greek
or any other way she can

This afternoon
she is neatly opiated
stumbling proudly
keeping the tilt
past the intoxicated street crowd

two dogs fucking
ranging
around her feet

and to look in those glassy eyes
one can see
her thinking

fuck me, one of you
stiff pricked bastards
fucking possess me

the poor old bitch in heat

nunto FORTY-FIVE

Dead.
decomposing body in the apartment
paraphernalia nearby
unrecognizable
seated in that angry chair

another god damned American rock star
spike in the arm

riding the big black horse of death

nunto FORTY-SIX

don't know how it ever really get to this point
where I'm standing on the front lawn
somewhere in Southern suburbia
with a Molotov cocktail in one hand
and a pitchfork in the other

covered in pig's blood
rearing back that right hand
and hurling that lightning bolt through
the plate glass front window
so it shatter
and light the living room on fire

and I'm leaping through the gasoline
hoping the pig's blood will keep my skin from burning
and I'm mostly naked
except for the jack boots

and screaming
here comes the fucking devil
here comes the fucking devil
here to kill you all

and the devil is in me
and i am the devil
the all original
the unmatchable
grand march fuck devil
with real fangs under this mask
out for blood and fire and
voodoo style vengeance

and we do it like this
me and Baron Samedi
'cause when you hate a fucker this bad
you got to do the fear right
so if we don't kill him tonight

his own heart
it'll do it for us

nunto FORTY-SEVEN

So lonely
that I hope
someone breaks in
here
do what they want

but maybe talk a bit
and hold me
touch my hands
touch my face when it's done

for I am old and thinking
will no one help me with this suffering?

The same soft cry
bound by night

framed by rain
and a desperation

so tired
so many years

how long have I been here?

nunto FORTY-EIGHT

watching the absinthe
curdle
with water
and menstrual blood

smoke bleeding out

girls talking about men

semen coagulating
alighting on unbroken wombs

nunto FORTY-NINE

I find myself
correcting people's grammar
these days

with a black marker
in the bathrooms
of places that sell beer
without brand names

the language of cock jokes
needs some guardian archangel
to ensure it's properly spoken

nunto FIFTY

i no longer believe anything that i am told

a pack of god damn liars
lulled into thinking
whatever comes out of my mouth is truth

christ
a nation unto god
what the fuck does that say for straight thinking?
bloody cultists and their mantras

look man
we're deluded and heavily armed
extremists in every sense of the word
rhetoric
hell bent on revenge and fast forward colonialization
via uncontested propaganda
which will obviously end
just like any other corpulent mule of an empire
imploding
under its own gargantuan weight

listen man
like any prophet, i can see the future
yes, i can see
a new charnel house
patrolled by the legions from the abyss
unshaven masses of johns and whores and
hairy, maladroit officers and judges and Lloyds
and corporate nightmares
gibbering madly and drooling and infecting those about us
screaming and ranting to the spirits of the winds

speak man
and i say holy snatch!
holy christ and the four fucking horsemen!
where the fuck is the word of god?

and the clammer of hoofbeats ring the bells of satori
like an old Priest emptying his bowels at the moment of his death
with a savage booming fart
that tears a bleeding asshole in the sky
and unleashes the poor old Beast of the Apocalypse

who promptly looks around at his intended meal
and vomits in disgust
before ducking his head beneath the waves
and fleeing in open panic
before the oncoming hordes
all the while muttering

shit on the cross, brother
shit on the fucking cross

and silence comes
thereafter that hums
before we all sober up a bit
and coyly ask ourselves

whatever does it mean to be American?
besides
a jihad against one's self?

BOOK IV

nunto FIFTY-ONE

An unfortunate incident
on my first day
attempting an office job

my bowels aren't ready for early rising
so I leave the company bathroom
smelling like a Romanian slaughter house
and bump into
the little tight-titted flytrap of a secretary
on the way out

her head torn back by the smell
she looks at me accusingly
and I
shamefaced
caught brown-handed
look down and start walking

I know
there's no day two
hell, I don't even go back to my desk.

just give up that notion for good
sell the shirt and suit jacket on the way home
buy a bottle of cheap rum, a notebook and red pen
and quit fucking kidding myself

nunto FIFTY-TWO

i was hoping to meet my brother
somewhere in this state

sometime around harvest
hoping to remember
his voice
and his laughter

maybe help to get Nat's out of
my head
but his wife's going to give birth
and he's unable to meet me

so here i sit in an oil slick overcoat
wearing a droopy John Deere farm hat
in yet another unnamed watering hole
snorting Jack Daniel's off
the upturned nipples of
chipped shot glasses

old friends that always show up
the Bourbon brothers
and their frail Russian comrades

always the same conversation repeated
that i can't fucking speak to
anymore

really need to detoxify
get off the nod and stop burning the oil

and i was thinking
it was essential to dilute this current rotting
with a few jokes and old stories
a vector of K's childhood laughter
and let it colour
instead of festering

some days, Nat
i wish your old uterus hadn't busted that afternoon
for i am
tired of the hustle

nunto FIFTY-THREE

my woman
naked on the carpet

lying there
as she is too stoned to consider
doing anything more immaculate

Full moon in the Nevada desert
too high to care
What?

what is said goes away
and floats later

nebulous
what really occurred

what was said
who threw the first punch
what was real

and what was fabrication

all we know is we both woke up
with black eyes
lying in a broken chair
piss all over the floor
semen in her hair

and mine

my half erect cock still stuck
in one of her glued up holes
and shit smeared on the wall like someone
threw it with intent to injure

a fine way to walk over a threshold
nervously rubbing these
rings on our fingers

but i guess

a house
is not a home
till you've spilled enough blood and semen and urine
in one place
to properly stain it your own

nunto FIFTY-FOUR

begging for a pussy bath
aren't you?
and know you'll get it 'cause
you know i
lean on women
like any other kind of drug

might stop taking this one in particular
for a few days
but like old Burroughs
i am a master addict
i cannot go for long without something in me

and if i cannot Fuck a woman
i'll Fuck a man
'cause the religion is Fucking
and maybe it's the drugs
and maybe it's just easier like that sometimes
'cause you can always find some codger homo
looking to hammer a piece of young ass

what can you do
old man
what can you do

nunto FIFTY-FIVE

Naked and drunk
face down on somebody's lawn

the high beams rolling past
squares slowing down and pointing

and I should be embarrassed
degraded derided de facto

but really

I'm young and I'm naked
and I'm drunk and running fast
and close to the ground and invincible
and my cock is half stiff
jangling back and forth like some
burnt log out of the mill chute
and I'm saying

the hell with all that
I'm made out of doggamn iron

and for tonight
and years to come

death cannot touch me
I am immortal

so put that on your cross and smoke it

nunto FIFTY-SIX

Eating of the dead
an old lover
with her stoneless eyes
rises up in dreams
while I lie there

etherized
beneath the sea
borne down by the chains of the Promethean rock

watching as the old buzzard
strips away
these poisoned organs

the taste of lingering flesh

nunto FIFTY-SEVEN

shadow of a knot
in big sky country
or whatever the fuck they're calling Texas these days
home of a hundred million handguns

a dangerous voice that visits
from time to time while I sit astride the horse
the Neural Machinist
an old Einsatzkommando

tough to decide which is more frightening
his crippled visage
or the fact that he visits

to tell me about the ethics of murder
how it is not necessarily wrong to kill at times
because wrong does not exist
it is a word made up by priests
and therefore does not apply to atheists like us

which is a frightening liberation
like the first time one hears and believes
that god is dead
a shadow on a cave wall, long like buddha
but nothing else

they walk in peace
a ring of Jews
a little tick and the bullet
blows their brains into the snow
and there is nothing else
for as a godless man
you know they know nothing else

there is no pain or suffering
no, it seems
the so-called wrong comes in letting them know
they will die before they are killed
setting upon them
a relentless terror in their last days or minutes
like the hour of fear on the Steppes at Babi Yar
or the twenty years spent in a Southern row of cells
populated with vagrants too depleted to afford their own lives

the civilized way as they call it now
not so much how I would do it
maybe my method is unheard of
the way
the impact of the bullet
is unheard by the shooter

death is human, my friend
but I always thought the taunting
inhuman
poor old Fyodor on the execution grounds
with his laughing riflemen
and still you call me atrocious

merciless barbarians
with your sanitized needles
and your silken ropes

and your holocaust
franchise for the poor

nunto FIFTY-EIGHT

I have a strong back to work with
and a stiff Cock

and that's what they're paying for
these days
that's what they're paying for
Nat

the real money

so that's what I'm working
making money on my back

but I'm not going
to tell that to a room of conspirators
in fact
I'm not going to tell anyone

burning it all, girl
photographs and letters

nunto FIFTY-NINE

odd what one thinks of
when cut deep
and bleeding badly

after a quick sort of knife fight
between me and an Arab who pulled
a pair of fucking linen scissors in the parking lot
behind the Gainford Motel
and started swinging like he was
one of Kurosawa's lost ronin
and all because I was swearing out loud at god's mother
and Toshiro thought I was talking to him

so now I'm holding my fingers together
watching Blood stream down the sink
wondering how I'm going to get sewed up
with no insurance, hell, no identity
and it's reminding me of the last time
I saw Blood in the sink

putting the fear of Blood in me

held still in one of those moments of brutal mortality
the fear over the Disease
'cause I fucked this crazy Bitch
who was a beautiful girl

but also
a drug addict
and an alcoholic
and we had a heated affair
for a couple of months

until I couldn't deal with the police
and her father threatening to kill me
and the razor blade incidents in the bathroom

and her phoning early in the mornings
saying
she didn't know where she was

'cause she was out all night
on a cocaine binge with some Cubans

she was a dirty fucked up Girl
who fucked a lot of guys
and I'm sure she was
raped once or twice

and had her own Death wishes
so what would she care if she was carrying

fucked her and a number of other
horrendous women
that I won't identify
because
I don't know their names

so accordingly
i could be dying quicker than we all intend
might not clear thirty-five
if that's the case
if that's the illness

so that's the fear i got
watching my own rancid Blood
curdling on porcelain i don't own
in a shitty hotel where people die every week

thinking senseless ironic thoughts
when they should be trying to think of someone to phone
who won't hang up when they realize
who it is on the other end

nunto SIXTY

after i finish fucking yet another
starched out
dry ass desert pussy

i know why i keep going back
why i am helpless
a child in the undertow
why i will return to her soon

because
nat's pussy is preternatural
a separate dimension

and every time i fuck her
it is like fucking the ocean
being covered up by deep water
staring up at
a young mermaid
with dripping thighs
spread open and rocking back
and forth
undulating with the tide

a welcome death by drowning
repeated
night after night
fathoms down
nothing but starlight and a faint unbroken moon
casting luminescent ribbons
to us through the waves

how peaceful to be crushed
under the pure atmospherics of water
dying that solemn little death every night
floating helpless in the void
mesmerized by the siren's song

nunto SIXTY-ONE

got the vein rising
smoking the dragon

All at once - street lights
Blink off in unison
[-morning]
City opens her eyes

cocksellers coming home
from a long night
of burning rod

and I hover on the edge
fleeing from demons

trying to touch
her
those unholy dark red lips
moist and cushiony
the kind that could
permanently damage a cock for any other woman.

lost

on the
Chinese horizon

nunto SIXTY-TWO

For the life of me
i cannot find a gun or a shiv anywhere
on a night like this with everything on the other side
and me with a real fucking death wish
to get there
get away from you
been staring off bridges and taunting oncoming trucks
been out all night walking the streets
fast
under the green haze

looking for a huge Iranian whore
who goes by the name Therese

I wanted her to crush me
to lie on me like a dead animal
and force the air from my lungs

she'd do it, too.
she's into shit like that
she would respect a man's wish
to die beneath her
a real old fashioned Middle East whore
a great great whore

but she is gone from the street
cooking in the House of D
or busy with a trick
or gone back to the desert to die

so I've had to settle for some large black
London bitch who don't understand
what I'm saying
and of course

by now I'm so triggerfucked
by the absinthe
there's no way to tell her
what i want is to die

nothing to do
but sit here mutely
with my cock in her mouth

wishing she'd lay me down
cover my face with her
enormous breasts

and let me gently suffocate
in darkness

nunto SIXTY-THREE

Don't give me that shit
bullfucker

I have a very clean
a very clear
picture of what the world is

and what we are in it

your god never existed in the first place

we're just dirty fucking animals
a bunch of god damned shaved apes
wearing ties

we fuck each other
we kill each other
and when it comes down to it
we'll fucking eat each other

how many times have I yelled this
violently drunk in one of the thousands
of urine spots
I've soiled myself in across this country
waking up with blackened eyes
bleeding assholes, strangers in the bed

and

still wondrous at the fact
that everyone is deaf to the words
that I speak

why can't any of you fucks
you castigating, plague ridden fucks
why can't you hear me?

this is what i cry in the stone rolling hours of the morning
when the bottle has stopped listening

the bluster meant to conceal
nervousness
that the bed is empty
that i probably can't stand this purgatory
much longer
that i am continuously thinking

fuck it all
fuck this exile
i am cracking open this tomb and
i am heading north tomorrow
where it is cold and pure
and the poison is
closer to my heart - a fresh gland

even though
i can't go home now
even though
i can't go home ever
even though all i want is
to wake up in the light of my home and fuck
and listen to her demure

for she won't ever say it
but there is a disgusting beauty
to our soiled love sheets
in the afternoon sun
an austerity of cum and blood and sweat
that we washed away
when we should have lain in that shroud
awhile longer

regrets turned over
masking what i have now
restlessness, insomnia, drunkenness and whores
and ghosts and nails to keep me company

burning paper
late in the unbreathing night

ready to break down
to shift paradigms
to hear true satori

ready for the chrysalis
to burst wide open
and allow me through
on jaded wings

about THE AUTHOR

Mingus Tourette was born and raised in western Canada. He is the author of *The Daily Mingus*, an online serial with a fanatical fan base.

Mingus Tourette still lives in the west, where he is working on his next novel. He is no longer married and has no children, to the best of his knowledge.

He signs his name:

Mingus Tourette
Emphatic Graphomaniac
Chronic Neologist
Thanaphobic Bastard
Purveyor of Fine Apostasy
Effervescent Fuckaroo
&
Notorious Drunkard, Esquire